Text © Mathew Price 1987
Illustrations © Errol Le Cain 1987
This edition published in the UK 2002 by Mathew Price Ltd
The Old Glove Factory, Bristol Road
Sherborne, Dorset DT9 4HP, UK
Printed in China
ISBN Hardback:1-84248-039-1
ISBN Paperback:1-84248-045-6

Mathew Price

THE CHRISTMAS STOCKINGS

Illustrated by Errol Le Cain

MATHEW PRICE LTD

It's Christmas Eve.
Santa Claus has come to fill
two little stockings with toys.
But there's no chimney.
How will he get down?
Can you help him?

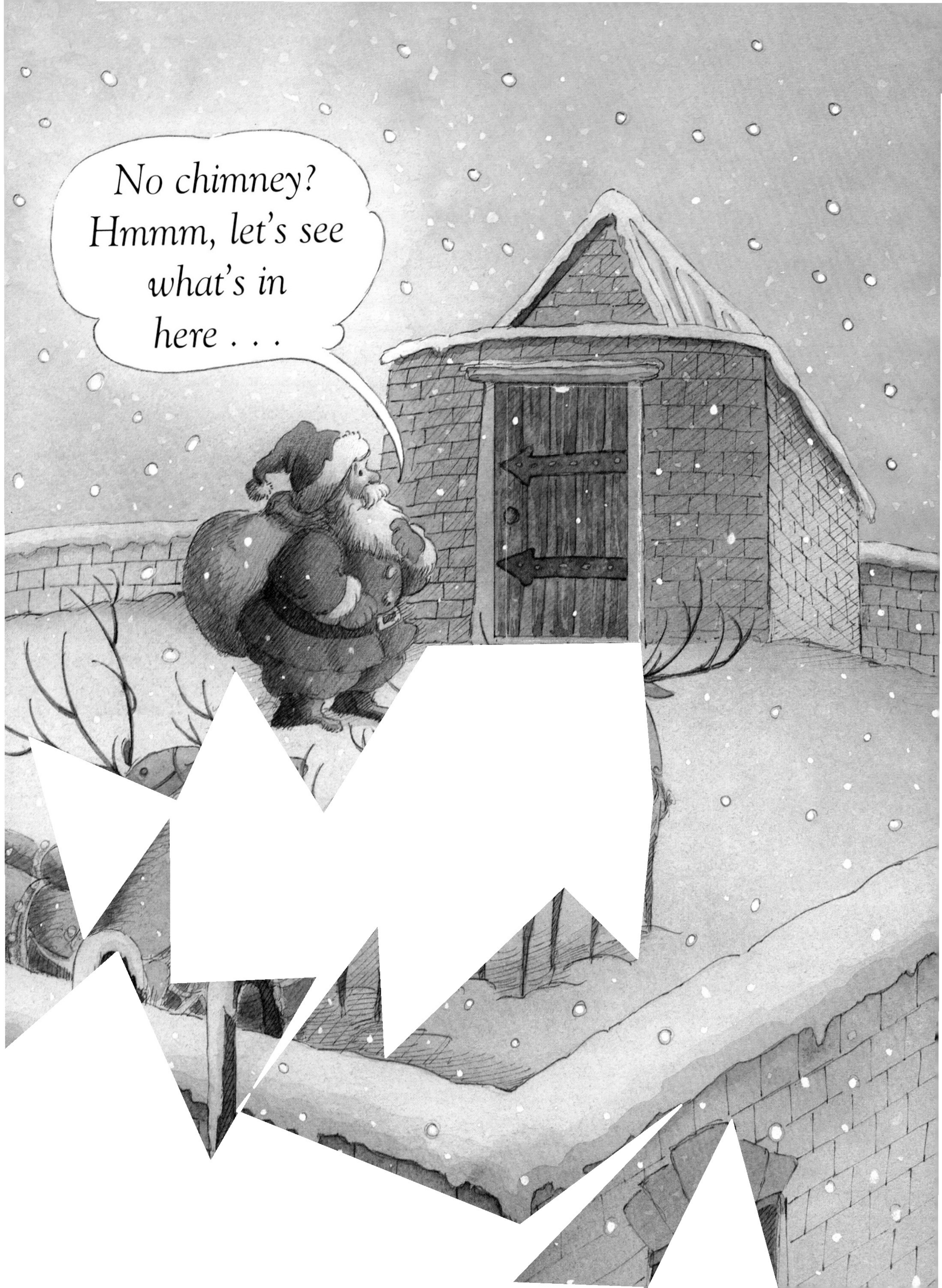
No chimney? Hmmm, let's see what's in here . . .

Well, he's inside the house.
But there are no stockings here.
Where can he go now?

Wrong again!

I hear music. Let's take a look . . .

There are still no stockings. We'll have to help him again. Can you find another door?

I love
parties!

A Christmas party! What fun.
But we can't stop here.
We have to find those stockings.
Where's the way out?

EXIT

I must get out of here before I'm sold.

Ouch! That was quite a drop! Now, what's this? A toy shop? Yes, it is. We'll never find the stockings here. Come on, Santa Claus, it's getting late.

There they are!